This is a story about **Tee** and **Mo**, a **little monkey** and his **monkey mum** who sometimes want to do **different things . . .** but **always** end up having **fun together**.

"**WOO-HOO!**"  shouts Tee,

bursting into Mo's room.

"**Time to wake up!**"

Tee *always loves* mornings,
but this one is **super special!**

Mo **doesn't** love mornings quite as much, **especially early ones.**

"Five **more** minutes . . ." she murmurs sleepily.

Mo's been **working** . . .

shopping . . .

cooking . . .

cleaning …

and **keeping** fit.

It's been a
busy week.

OO-AH!

But Tee **can't** wait five minutes. He bounces on Mo's head.

BOING!
BOING!
BOING!

"You haven't **forgotten**, have you?" he asks.
Mo slowly opens one eye.

"**Forgotten what?**" she asks.

"**Picnic day!**
You **promised!**"
Tee reminds her.

"Are we **ready**
to **go?**"

No, Mo is not
ready to go.

She **forgot!**

While Mo makes them both breakfast, Tee makes them both a plan.

He's **good** at plans.

"Okay, here's the plan," he says. "I'm going to do . . .

running . . .

then jumping . . .

then **eating**
and **drinking**.
Then **playing**,
then **more playing** ...

then EVEN MORE
PLAYING!"

"That's **a lot** of **playing!**" Mo comments. She puts away the breakfast things and grabs her bag.

"**YAY!**" shouts Tee excitedly.

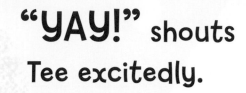

"Are we ready to go now?

Are we?

Are we?"

Mo hands Tee a delicious-looking sandwich.

"We've got the **snack,** we've got the **keys** and **now** we're ready to go!" he says.

"**Uh-oh,**"
replies Mo.

"I don't think so . . ."

"We can't go **without a drink!**" she cries.

Tee and Mo have got **the keys**,

they've got **the drink**.

they've got **the snack**,

Surely *now* they're **ready to go?**

"**And a rug,**"
adds Mo,

"to sit on at the park!"

They **must**
be ready to
go **now.**

Uh-oh!
That'll be a no.

Tee's forgotten his ball!

And Mo grabs a book
– just in case.

Look at Tee and Mo – they're **absolutely** ready to go!
Picnic day, here they come . . .

Wait!
Just one last thing –
Tee's drum.

A picnic's *not* a picnic
without a drum,

right?

Finally, Tee and Mo are ready to go!

They've got
the keys.

They've got
the snack.

They've got
the drink.

They've got
the map.

They've got
the rug.

They've got
the ball.

They've got **the book.**

They've got **the drum.**

But they've also got a **very heavy** bag.

OO-AH!

But don't worry.
Tee has got a plan!

He **runs** . . .

he **jumps** . . .

he **unpacks** . . .

he gets **snacks** . . .

. . . and relaxes.

"We've been **so busy** getting ready that I think we're going to

stay at home,"

Tee explains between mouthfuls of sandwich.

"Great plan, clever Tee!" replies Mo, picking up her book.

"Now this is a **perfect** picnic day."

OO-AH!

Are We Ready to Go?

Are we ready to go?
Uh-oh!
Are we ready to go?
I don't think so!

CHORUS

I think we've forgotten the keys.
We've got the keys!
And now we're ready to go!

CHORUS

We might need a snack.
We've got the snack!
We've got the keys!
And now we're ready to go!

CHORUS

Oh, we can't go without a drink.
We've got the drink!
We've got the snack!
We've got the keys!
And now we're ready to go!

CHORUS

Oh, we must remember the map.
We've got the map!
We've got the drink!
We've got the snack!
We've got the keys!
And now we're ready to go!

CHORUS

We need a rug to sit on in the park.
We've got the rug!
We've got the map!
We've got the drink!
We've got the snack!
We've got the keys!
And now we're ready
 to go!

CHORUS

Oh, Tee, you've forgotten your ball!
We've got the ball!
We've got the rug!
We've got the map!
We've got the drink!
We've got the snack!
We've got the keys!
And now we're ready to go!

CHORUS

You might want a book to read if
  you get bored.
We've got the book!
We've got the ball!
We've got the rug!
We've got the map!
We've got the drink!
We've got the snack!
We've got the keys!
And now we're ready to go!

CHORUS

We definitely need your drum.
We've got the drum!
We've got the book!
We've got the ball!
We've got the rug!
We've got the map!
We've got the drink!
We've got the snack!
We've got the keys!

And NOW WE'RE READY TO GO!
Yes, we're finally ready to go!
But we're so tired from getting
  ready to go,
That I think we're going to
  stay at home.

Turn the page to play the song using our **special QR code!**

Scan with your phone
to hear the original song
sung by Lauren Laverne

www.harpercollinschildrensbooks.co.uk/teeandmo